KING WORM JACK

BY NATALIE GORDON

For Isla

Also available by Natalie Gordon for readers aged 9+

Mr. Nobody

First published in 2022
by Natalie Gordon

British Library Cataloguing-in-Publication data
A catalogue record for this book is available from the British Library

ISBN: 978-1-7397436-0-4

Every effort has been made to trace the copyright holders and obtain permission to reproduce this material.

Designed and typeset by
Carnegie Scotforth Book Production

Printed and bound by Severnprint

For more information about the author, please visit www.nataliegordon.co.uk

Chapter 1

"Hey, look! It's just like you!" Seb held up a long, wrinkly worm between his thumb and forefinger and waved it in front of Jack. "Ugly, slimy and useless at football."

He threw it into Jack's face. Seb was too close and too quick for Jack to jump out of the way, so the cold, clammy body of the worm smacked against Jack's cheek, and fell into the flowerbed at his feet. Seb picked up his football from the same flowerbed and kicked it back onto the lawn.

"Wor-m, wor-m, wor-m" chanted Seb as he dribbled the football down the garden and kicked it into the top left-hand corner of the net. "GOAAAL!" he yelled, sliding on his knees with his fists clenched in the air above him.

Starting secondary school, had made Seb even more mean than usual. And to make it worse, their mum and dad never seemed to notice, even though it was REALLY obvious.

"It's supper time!" shouted their mum from the back door. "Time to come in and wash your hands." She paused, staring at Jack. "Especially you, Jack. What ARE you doing in the flowerbed?"

Jack was on his hands and knees trying to find the worm. He wanted to make sure it was okay, but he thought it had maybe already wriggled away. Lucky worm. Sometimes he thought he'd like to wriggle away where no one could find *him*. Especially where Seb couldn't find him.

Jack sighed and got up, brushing the mud off his knees. Max came meowing up to him, rubbing himself against his trousers.

"Cats are useless," sneered Seb as he walked past. "He's not meowing 'cos he likes you; he's just hungry. Bet you wish you had a dog. Dogs are proper pets."

Right then, Scarlet, Seb's dog, came bounding out of the house and ran up to Seb, woofing madly, like she'd really missed him in the ten minutes they'd been outside.

Jack *had* wished he could have his own dog, but because they already had one, he wasn't allowed one. His parents had offered to get him a cat instead for his 8th birthday.

He hadn't really wanted a cat, but when they went to the pet rescue place in the summer holidays, Max had walked straight up to Jack, and chosen him. He'd rubbed his nose against Jack's shin, sat down, looked up at him and meowed, like he was asking to come home with him. Jack's resistance to cats melted away right then. He just knew that Max was going to be a zillion times better than any dog.

"Jack! I won't ask you again! Stop daydreaming, get out of the flowerbed, come in for supper and do NOT leave a trail of mud behind you!"

Jack walked slowly towards the house. The other thing that he wished, apart from being able to wriggle away like the wrinkly worm, was that he was an only child, like his best friend, Sally.

Sally had her parents all to herself. They had nobody to compare her to, so she could be really bad at maths, but she'd be the best child in their house at maths. She was lucky. Actually, she was very clever too, so she'd never be bad at maths. The only bad thing in Sally's life as far as Jack could see, was their teacher, Mr. Prickles, and he was bad in *everybody's* life.

He'd told his mum how horrible Mr. Prickles was, but he knew she didn't believe him. When he'd been Seb's teacher, Seb had loved him. And Seb had won the county creative writing competition that year with a stupid story about a boy and his dog. So, of course, his parents and Seb all thought that Mr. Prickles was an amazing teacher. It was just one more reason why they thought Jack was useless. Useless at football, useless at maths, useless at stories, useless at everything.

"Meow!" Max ran round Jack's legs and into the house, leaving little muddy pawprints behind him.

"Jack!" yelled his mum. "Get that cat out of here!"

Chapter 2

Jack was in a tunnel, and it was dark and very narrow, but he didn't mind. In fact, he loved it because he found he could slip along it really easily. He kept going towards the archway he could see at the end. He could hear a very annoyed, high-pitched voice and he hurried along the tunnel to hear what was going on.

"This is absolutely ridiculous! I am NOT supposed to be in this hole. I am a bird. You are a worm. You cannot pull me down here. Let me go immediately!" squeaked the voice.

"Well, I did pull you down here, so I guess you're wrong," replied a low, lazy sounding voice that then started to chuckle. "Hey everyone, what would you like for supper?"

"We want bird! We want bird! We want yummy, scrummy, roasted bird!"

The chanting was so loud, it made Jack's tunnel shake and he reached out to hang on to the sides of the tunnel. Or at least he tried to reach out, but he found that he didn't have any arms. In fact, he didn't have any legs either. Horrified, Jack looked down at himself and saw a long, wrinkled, slimy brown body of... A WORM!!!

He *must* be dreaming, surely? He remembered that he'd been doodling in his secret sketchpad just before he went to sleep. He'd drawn a picture of a worm, wearing a crown, in charge of an army of worms who'd caught a bird for supper. They were like super worms with special powers.

He'd shown his sketch to Max who had purred his approval and rubbed his nose on it before curling up next to him on his pillow. It was the first time Jack had let Max sleep on his bed with him. His mum would go mad if she knew.

The tunnel started to shake as the chanting began again.

"We want bird! We want bird! We want..."

Jack tumbled out of the tunnel and into a large room with a ceiling shaped like the inside of a cathedral roof. It seemed to have a large, bird shaped hole in the middle of it. In front of him, was a rectangular, wooden dining table and, strapped to the top of it, was a furious looking robin with a very puffed-up chest. Around the table sat ten worms with napkins around their necks, who stopped midway through their chant when Jack appeared. They started to bow to him, and one worm wriggled over to him.

"King Worm Jack! It's an honour to have you, Your Majesty. Chief Worm Rodney at your service. Will you join us for roasted bird?"

Chapter 3

Jack was confused. He looked at the worms and then at the bird. They all seemed to be waiting for his answer.

"Um, well, I mean, um..."

Before he could work out what to say, the bird coughed and started to speak, "If I may, Your Majesty, I would like to say something."

Jack nodded.

"Your Majesty" said the bird, dabbing at her eyes with her wing feathers, "my babies are all alone and they are hungry. They will starve to death if I don't get back to them. I'm ever so sorry, but lovely juicy worms are the best food for baby birds. I promise I will never come back again — if I could just take one incy wincy worm back with me. Just one for my poor darling starving babies."

The robin started to cry, peeping out at Jack from under her wing every now and then.

"If I may also say a few words, Your Majesty?" demanded Chief Worm Rodney. The other worms were shuffling angrily in their seats and glaring at the robin. Jack nodded, pleased that he didn't have to say anything yet.

"Your Majesty, this bird is a murderer, and we demand that she be killed and eaten as punishment."

"Yeah, kill her!"

"She's a menace!"

"She's a meanie!"

"She's a murderer!"

"She's very tasty looking, too!"

Everyone was staring at Jack, waiting for his answer. He began to wish he could just wriggle away unnoticed, but they clearly thought he was in charge, just like the worm in his drawing.

So, he cleared his throat and stood up taller. It was then that he felt the weight of a crown upon his head for the first time. The taller he stood, the braver he felt, as if the crown was pouring courage and wisdom into his mind.

 draw here

"I hereby declare that birds should eat berries and worms should eat mud." Jack smiled at everyone, but no one smiled back. He added hastily, "juicy, red berries for birds and maybe some raisins too, and some big, fat green leaves mixed in with the mud for the worms." He stopped, feeling less brave than before, but to his relief, everyone cheered. The robin was released and saluted him with her wing before she flew out of the hole in the ceiling.

Jack felt brilliant, better than he'd ever felt before. Maybe he could order the worms to carry his brother away for a day? Then he could be an only child like Sally and be the best child in his house at EVERYTHING. It was only a dream after all, so no one would be worried about Seb.

Jack gathered the worms around him and spoke in his best King voice.

"As the King, I command you to take my brother away for a day."

Chapter 4

Jack's eyes snapped open. A wet nose was nudging his cheek. Max meowed loudly and head-butted Jack's cheek. Jack turned over on to his side to give him a proper stroke, but Max jumped down on to the floor, meowed again and walked over to the door. He stopped, looked over his shoulder at Jack and meowed for the third time.

"SEB! Get up NOW! Don't just lie there!"

Jack sprang out of bed. Why was mum yelling at Seb? He followed Max out on to the landing and tried to see past his mum into Seb's room. It was tricky because she was standing in the doorway. Max rubbed himself against Jack's legs, insistently, like he did when he wanted to be picked up, so Jack lifted him up.

"MUUUM! I can't get out of bed! HELP!" screamed Seb.

Jack's dad ran up the stairs and pushed past Jack to get to the doorway.

"What on earth has happened here? Where did all those *worms* come from? Seb, come on, out of there, now!"

Jack peered under his dad's arm and saw a seething mass of worms covering his brother's floor and wriggling their way up his bed legs. Seb looked terrified. Jack backed away, all of a sudden feeling a little weird, like his thoughts had got tangled up into a big knot inside his head. Max purred softly.

Jack didn't understand. It was only a dream he'd had last night, wasn't it? He thought back to the instructions he'd given to the worms to carry his brother away. He hadn't even realised there were so many of them.

Jack watched as his dad waded through the worms into Seb's room, picked him up from his bed and plonked him on the landing. Jack hoped he hadn't squashed any of the worms. Seb's dog, Scarlet, was whimpering outside the bedroom. Mum grabbed Seb and pushed him towards the stairs.

"We'll have to get a number for pest control and call them out," said his dad. "There are just so many of them. Seb, what *have* you been collecting? There must be something in your room that's attracting them. I've never seen anything like it."

Seb shook his head indignantly. "It's not me. I haven't done anything."

"Well, there must be something in your room because they haven't gone anywhere else, have they? I wonder how they got in there. I've never heard of a worm infestation before."

Jack couldn't help smirking. Seb saw him.

"It's him! It's Jack! He's done it!"

"I have not! How would I have made all those worms get in your room?"

Max meowed and looked at Jack. Jack could have sworn he saw Max wink. Actually, he was sure he'd seen him wink last night, too, just before he fell asleep. Scarlet growled at Max, who arched his back and swiped his paw at her. Just a warning swipe.

The worms started to slither out of Seb's room and across the landing. Jack stepped back into his doorway. His mum screamed.

"Ugh! They're everywhere! Quick, downstairs!"

"I'll get a bucket and a dustpan and brush. Maggie, you find a number for pest control. Jack! Don't just sit there, come downstairs!" yelled his dad.

Dad, Seb and Mum (known usually as 'your mum' or as 'Maggie' when dad was cross or 'Mags' when Dad was being lovesick soppy) all raced downstairs. Jack stayed where he was, thinking. The worms were nearly at the top of the stairs.

What if he were to tell them to stop? After all, last night he had been King Worm Jack, so maybe they would listen to him. He cleared his throat loudly. The army of worms stopped at the top of the stairs and in one movement turned around to face him. Jack whispered urgently,

"I command you to stop. Mission accomplished. You may return to base."

The army of worms bowed as one and slithered down the stairs and out of the house. Max meowed and winked at Jack. It was definitely a wink.

Seb hadn't been carried away for the day, but Jack didn't care about that now. He felt a tingle of excitement fizzing down his spine. Something very weird was going on and he LOVED it!

Chapter 5

Jack was sitting at his table in the classroom and the daylight was streaming in through the windows, surrounding Jack in a rectangle of warmth. He was exhausted after last night's wormy adventures and his eyes kept drooping shut to the sound of Mr. Prickles' voice droning on in the background, like a lawnmower humming in the distance. As his eyes tried to shut again, Jack gave in and let them, just to rest them for a bit. After all, the lesson hadn't quite started yet.

The classroom disappeared. He was King Worm Jack in command of his army of worms. They were advancing on the enemy. The enemy was Seb and his dog, Scarlet. Jack was on Max's back and they were charging towards Seb and Scarlet when, all of a sudden, they were stopped by the big, bad, prickly giant hedgehog.

"Jack! Wake up!"

The giant hedgehog was shaking his shoulder. The worm army was gathering behind Jack, ready to slither forwards and capture the enemy.

"Jack! Stand up!"

As the giant hedgehog hauled him to his feet, Sally poked him with the sharp point of her pencil. Jack opened one eye and used it to glare at Sally. It hurt where she'd poked him. She was supposed to be his best friend. She mouthed, 'sorry' at him.

"I do believe your friend was trying to wake you up," the giant hedgehog said between thin, tight lips.

Jack glanced back at Sally. She nodded in agreement with the hedgehog, who he could now see looked very much like Mr. Prickles.

Jack rubbed his eyes, trying to rub the sleep away. He couldn't believe he'd actually fallen asleep in class. "Sorry, Mr. Prickles," he mumbled.

"I should think you are. Five star jumps, now!"

"Pardon?" Jack stared at Mr. Prickles. He'd gone mad. He couldn't really expect him to do five star jumps in front of the whole class, could he?

"You heard me! Five star jumps! That will wake you up."

There was some sniggering from the rest of the class.

"QUIET! Otherwise you will ALL be doing star jumps."

Jack tentatively did his first star jump, feeling his face burn red hot with embarrassment.

"Put some effort into it, otherwise you'll be doing ten!"

Jack felt a big knot in his throat and blinked back humiliated tears as he did four more star jumps, all the time staring at the floor.

"Right, now sit back down and concentrate on your work. If you fall asleep in my class again, or fail to pay attention, it will be ten star jumps. Do I make myself clear?"

"Yes, Mr. Prickles," Jack mumbled.

Mr. Prickles glared at him, walked back to his desk and sat down, his bushy eyebrows frowning.

Mr. Prickles' eyebrows looked just like those poisonous furry caterpillars Jack sometimes found in the garden when he was bug hunting.

If Seb found him searching for worms or caterpillars or any other creature, sometimes he would stamp on them and squash them, just to annoy Jack. He wouldn't dare stamp on a caterpillar on Mr. Prickles' face though. Jack winced and screwed up his face in pain and sympathy for the caterpillar *and* Mr. Prickles.

Sally kicked him under the table, and he winced for real, bending down to rub his shin where she'd kicked him. "Jack!" she hissed, pulling a face at him with her finger to her lips, before pointing at Mr. Prickles.

Jack looked over and found Mr. Prickles glaring at him, one bushy caterpillar eyebrow raised and the other straight as a ruler. Jack swallowed hard, and looked down at his numeracy worksheet, where the numbers seemed to dance around and mock him. He could almost hear them, whispering, "useless" to each other as he picked up his pencil.

"Jack Wrigglesworth! I've had enough of you today already! I want you to sit right here for the rest of the day!"

Mr. Prickles pointed at the desk in front of his, which was in pretty much constant use in Mr. Prickles' class for the kids he'd "had enough of". Jack picked up his stuff, walked slowly over to the dreaded desk and slid into the chair, wishing he could just keep sliding off the chair and disappear into a worm tunnel.

"Maybe with a bit of concentration, you might make sense of your numbers for once."

Jack said nothing, but wiped some stray spit off his cheek, which had come flying out of Mr. Prickles' mouth (the main reason why everyone hated being made to sit there). He smoothed out the worksheet in front of him, took a deep breath and stared at question one. It was going to be a really, really long day.

Chapter 6

When his mum picked him up at the end of the day, and asked how school had been, Jack shrugged and responded with, "Okay."

"Okay? Is that it?"

"Yep."

Jack kicked a pebble along the pavement.

"So, what did you do today?"

"Can't remember."

"What? You can't remember anything at all?"

Jack shook his head. They walked along in silence for a bit.

"Is it Mr. Prickles again?"

Jack nodded. Mum sighed and put her arm round his shoulders.

"You know, I'm sure he's not that bad. Maybe you just need to concentrate a bit more in class."

Jack pulled away and kicked another pebble even harder. It landed in the gutter.

"It's not me, it's him."

"Well, okay. All I'm saying is that he used to be Seb's favourite teacher, and I've only ever heard people say how brilliant he is. If he really is as bad as you say he is, then either something happened to him over the summer holidays to change him completely, or you're doing something that winds him up."

Jack didn't answer.

Later that night in bed, Jack thought about what his mum had said. Something must have happened to Mr. Prickles in the holidays. Jack wasn't winding him up. He wasn't the only one in the class Mr.

Prickles was mean to. In fact, Jack couldn't think of a single child that Mr. Prickles had said anything nice to since the start of term.

He pulled out his sketchpad from under his pillow and drew Mr. Prickles with the biggest, hairiest caterpillar eyebrows you've ever seen. Then he surrounded him with question marks. What had happened in the summer holidays to turn Mr. Prickles from a brilliant teacher into a horrible, terrible teacher?

He slid the sketchpad back under his pillow and snuggled down under the duvet. Max jumped onto the bed and curled up next to him on his pillow, purring loudly. Jack scratched him between his ears.

"What do you think, Max? What if something has happened to turn Mr. Prickles nasty? What if we could find out? Imagine if we could just somehow get inside his mind and read his thoughts."

Jack sighed. That would be awesome, but was, of course, impossible.

"Night, night, Max."

He gave Max one final scratch between his ears. Jack could have sworn that Max winked and sent a zizz of light flashing across the duvet. A zizz was like a flash, but better.

Chapter 7

Jack woke up and found himself standing in a small, airy room with an arched roof. In front of him was a heavy-looking door, which was made out of planks of thick orange-brown wood. There were a few wet patches of green stuff on the door, like algae, Jack thought. There was a doorknocker in the shape of a hedgehog.

The light was coming from behind him. He turned around and saw two low tunnels, which acted like car headlights, because the daylight was shining through them on to the wooden door. He was standing in the middle of one of the beams of light. Standing next to him in the other beam was Chief Worm Rodney.

Rodney grinned at him and bowed. "Phew! I thought you were going to stand there forever, daydreaming. Shall we get started?"

If Jack had been able to scratch his head, he would have done. It helped him to think, but he was a worm again, so he didn't have any hands. Being a worm was good if you liked sliding, but it was rubbish if you needed to actually do anything else, like scratch. He had no idea where he was, or why he was here.

"Um, Rodney, where are we?"

Rodney doubled over and laughed as if Jack had just told the best joke ever. It made Jack feel uncomfortable, like when everyone else in the class is laughing and you don't know why, so you start to think that everyone is laughing at you. He frowned. "What's so funny?"

Rodney was having uncontrollable fits of giggles and reached out with his hands to support himself on the door.

Jack couldn't take his eyes off Rodney's hands.

"Where did your hands come from?" Jack exclaimed.

Rodney abruptly stopped laughing and stared at Jack, as if he were mad. "Are you feeling okay, Your Majesty?"

Jack wanted to kick something in frustration, but of course, he didn't have any feet, so he couldn't. "No, I'm not! I don't understand what's going on and why you now have hands and I don't."

"Well, I undid my wormsie, of course."

"Your wormsie?"

"Er...yes. Look." Rodney slithered over, much like mermaids would walk if they did walk, Jack thought. Rodney reached over and unfastened something at Jack's neck and then Jack felt air touching his skin as his wormsie unravelled, like a banana skin. Or rather, like a wormsie. Awesome.

"But I don't understand. How do you get it undone if your hands are zipped in?"

"I use my mouth, silly. Um, I mean, Your Majesty."

Jack had forgotten that he was King. He stood up straighter, to feel more king-like, and then he reached up and adjusted his crown on his head with his HANDS. It still didn't make sense though. Surely he would have seen their hands before? He asked Rodney.

"Oh no, we only get them out when we really need to. It's easier to move along the tunnels you see, without any arms and hands. And they can be distracting, if you wave them around when you talk."

Rodney was still looking at him curiously. He supposed, as their King, he should know this stuff. He thought about what Rodney had said. He'd seen the bobsleigh in the Olympics on telly. He guessed being a worm in a wormsie might be a bit like that in the tunnels. You'd be able to go really fast.

"Anyway, Your Majesty, shall we get on?"

"Get on where?"

"Into Mr. Prickles' brain, of course."

Chapter 8

Jack pinched himself to see if he was dreaming. "Ouch!" That hurt; it must be real. No one would ever believe him though, not even Sally.

Jack reached out for the hedgehog doorknocker and let it bang back onto the door. It echoed around the tiny room. He swallowed nervously.

A hatch in the door opened up and a glistening green blob with a small scrunched-up face spoke to them. Well, it was more of a squeak.

"Yes?" the blob demanded crossly.

Jack cleared his throat and said in his best Kingly voice, "We'd like to come in, please."

"Password, please."

Oh. Jack looked at Rodney, who shrugged.

"Um, I'm afraid we don't know the password."

The blob shouted behind him to someone, "THEY DON'T KNOW THE PASSWORD." Then he turned back to them, "You'll have to wait then, until Barry gets here."

Just then, a bigger, slimier green blob shoved the first blob out of the way and squeaked, "What's all this then? No password? Name please!"

And it was then that Jack realised what the glistening green blobs were — real living, breathing bogies — bogeymen! The two tunnels behind him were the nostrils and these bogeymen were guarding the entrance to Mr. Prickles' brain.

draw here

"It's King Worm Jack and Chief Worm Rodney, here to inspect Mr. Prickles' brain. We are on an urgent mission and it's extremely important that you let us in," announced Rodney.

As Rodney was talking, Jack puffed his chest out, to make himself look important. Then, he frowned and did his best 'very important grown-up, with very important things to do' look.

"Well, I'm sorry," said Barry the bogeyman, "but you still need a password. Tell you what, I'll give you a clue. What do hedgehogs do in winter?"

Jack jumped up and down, excitedly. "I know this one!" he shouted. "Hibernate!"

The door creaked open, and Jack wriggled in with Rodney beside him. They were now in an enormous cave-like room with a choice of four doors, all with signs on them. What if he opened the wrong one? Or even worse, what if he opened one, went through and then couldn't find his way back again? Jack shuddered. He didn't fancy getting lost in Mr. Prickles' brain.

Which door should they pick? Jack scratched his head and started to read the signs out loud.

"'Memories'. Well, I guess we could look in there and see if there are any bad memories that make him grumpy. What do you think, Rodney?"

"Excellent plan, Your Majesty. And maybe we could find some good memories to make him happy again."

Jack nodded thoughtfully, "Good idea." He carried on reading the other door signs. "'Bodyworks'. Well, I guess that's all about how he makes his body move and how he gets his blood to go round. We did that in one of his lessons, actually. You know, how veins take blood away from your heart and arteries take blood to your heart."

Rodney yawned.

"No, seriously, it's really interesting. Did you know that if you accidently cut an artery, you bleed LOADS." Jack paused, thoughtful for a moment. "I guess it's probably different for worms. I can find out though, and let you know."

Rodney was ignoring him and reading the sign on the next door, "'Brainworks'. Maybe we could get in here and change his thoughts?"

That did sound like an interesting idea, but Jack had already seen the door he HAD to go through: 'Eyebrow Control'. Ha! He knew it! Mr. Prickles' eyebrows were so massive and hairy, they had to have a room all to themselves!

"Rodney, look! 'Eyebrow Control'. Come on, let's go in!"

Jack slid over to the door and heaved it open.

Chapter 9

Jack and Rodney slipped inside the door and stood and looked around in awe. Jack couldn't wait to describe it to Sally. He didn't know much about sailing, but he imagined it might look something like this. It was as if he and Rodney were standing on the deck of a ship.

High above him were the eyebrows, massive bushy things that resembled hairy caterpillars. Actually, they WERE hairy caterpillars. There were ropes attached to the caterpillar eyebrows. That was really mean, thought Jack: it was like they were prisoners.

At the end of each rope, were two rainbow-coloured squidgy creatures. Jack stared at them, trying to work out exactly what they were. The bottom half of them was much fatter than the top half. They glistened in the light. On the floor around them, were little puddles. Then he got it: teardrops! They were teardrop creatures! Awesome!

Sitting high up, at the same height as the caterpillar eyebrows was a teardrop holding a megaphone. It was yelling at the other teardrops, telling them how to control the eyebrows.

"Right eyebrow team: pull down on the left and hoist up on the right! Left eyebrow team: Up! Down! Up! Down!"

The teardrops looked like they were enjoying themselves, because every time they pulled the rope, their bottom half lifted off the ground and they swung around at the ends of the rope, grinning.

Jack thought that these eyebrows must control the eyebrows on the outside of Mr. Prickles' head somehow, almost like they

 *draw here*

were magnets either side of a piece of card. Jack touched his own eyebrows. His were definitely not like caterpillars. They were more like the frayed bits at the end of his jumper sleeve. He frowned, wondering what *was* inside his head. Maybe it was more like a jumble sale. Maybe he'd got the leftover bits that no one else wanted and that was why he was no good at maths. Perhaps the maths bit of his brain was second hand? That made a lot of sense.

Jack was wondering what else might be second hand inside his head, and whether Seb had got all the new shiny parts, when he heard shouting from one of the teardrop teams.

"Get him off!"

"What's he doing?"

"Sound the alarm! Intruders!"

Rodney was slithering up one of the ropes, waving to Jack. Just as he reached the top, an alarm sounded, like the school fire alarm, and a flashing red light engulfed the whole room.

The teardrop in charge started to yell through its megaphone, "Left eyebrow! Shake that rope! Get him off!"

"Your Majesty, they really are caterpillars! I'm going to set them free!" Rodney shouted down to Jack from the caterpillar he had reached and was now stroking. Every time he touched it, it twitched and trembled and lifted the teardrops at the end of the ropes off the floor. Soon teardrops were flying around the room, clinging onto their ropes, squealing in panic.

Rodney was trying his best to calm the caterpillar down, while, at the same time, trying to untie the knots that held him captive in the ropes. Finally, he did it, and as that caterpillar wriggled away, Rodney swung on the rope across to the other caterpillar, who was jiggling about excitedly and flinging the teardrops at the ends of their ropes around the room.

"I've set one free, Your Majesty. I'll just let this one go!"

As Rodney yelled down to Jack, the door burst open and two bogeymen came in, armed with what looked like giant water guns. Jack shouted at Rodney, "Get down now! We have to go!" But it was too late.

The bogeymen fired their guns at Rodney and squirted him with...snot. Disgusting, green, gloopy snot. Rodney was covered and pretty soon, so was the caterpillar. It quivered, and seemed to let out a little squeak but then, as Rodney managed to untie the last knot, it crawled away too. Jack couldn't see where to, because there was slimy snot being fired all over the place and the teardrop creatures and Rodney were soon dripping with it. Only Jack had escaped the slime.

The chief teardrop was shouting, "Idiots! That stuff dries and sticks. It's going to take hours to get this place clean. You're too late anyway — the eyebrows are gone! Guards! Take these intruders and get out now! And you lot: stop swinging around on those ropes!"

Jack gazed anxiously up at Rodney as the teardrops slid to the ends of their ropes and dripped onto the floor. Rodney slithered down one of the ropes with difficulty, since he was encrusted in dried snot. Then the bogeymen pointed their guns at Jack. "Out of here, quick march!"

He shuffled out, followed by Rodney, who left a green trail behind him. Jack tried to imagine Mr. Prickles without eyebrows, but it was really hard. He tried to picture him looking cross about losing his eyebrows, but without them, Mr. Prickles wouldn't look nearly as cross. Eyebrows, Jack realised, were very helpful in letting you know how people felt.

Chapter 10

For once, Jack couldn't wait to get to school the next day. He wanted to tell Sally all about his night-time adventures, but when he walked into the classroom, he knew something was wrong. It was as if the class was collectively holding down the lid on a whole trouble-load of laughter.

"Sit down and be quiet!" Mr. Prickles yelled. But he yelled it, looking down at his desk.

Sally nudged Jack and whispered to him, "Look, he must have shaved his eyebrows!"

Jack felt faint. He stared at Mr. Prickles, but Mr. Prickles was still looking down at his desk. He hadn't meant anything bad to happen last night. He should have stopped Rodney.

Sally nudged him, "Hey, can you see? He's got no eyebrows left. Maybe his wife shaved them off for a joke when he was asleep." She stifled a giggle. Jack's head was pounding. He needed some fresh air. He stumbled to his feet but just as he stood up, he felt something brush past his cheek. Bang! A rubber hit Mr. Prickles' face right where his eyebrows should have been.

The rubber pinged off Mr. Prickles and landed on the floor. The whole class gasped. Jack was still on his feet, too scared to move. No one said a word. They all waited, but nothing happened. Then, very slowly, Mr. Prickles looked up, and glared at Jack. With his pointy nose and short spiky hair, Mr. Prickles reminded Jack of a hedgehog: a furious hedgehog, hungry for worms. Mr. Prickles' pointy nose twitched as he walked towards Jack's table. Jack sank back down into his chair.

Mr. Prickles still hadn't said a word. Jack looked up at him nervously and then quickly looked back down at the table. It was true: his eyebrows *had* gone. Well, nearly gone: instead of thick, bushy eyebrows, he had a thin, mean line above each eye.

"Have you had a good look, Jack?" asked Mr. Prickles very quietly.

"Um, yes, I mean, no. I, um..."

"Out."

Jack was confused, "Pardon?"

"Get out of my classroom. Now."

"But, where...?"

"You will go to Mrs. Root and you will tell her that you are a nasty, rude little boy. You will tell her that I do not want you in my classroom for the rest of the day."

Jack got up, feeling his cheeks burning right up to his ears. It wasn't fair. He hadn't done anything. Well, not today anyway. He hadn't thrown the rubber.

"But, Mr. Prickles, that's not fair. Jack didn't do it," protested Sally.

"It is perfectly fair, Sally. No child in my classroom EVER throws things at a teacher, or anyone else for that matter. Do I make myself clear?"

Sally bit her lip and nodded.

Jack burst out, "It wasn't me. I didn't throw the rubber."

"OUT!" Mr. Prickles' nose twitched, and his eyes glinted in the light coming through the windows. Jack got up and half ran, half stumbled to the door. Part of him was relieved to be out of the classroom, but part of him was really worried. If he could do that to Mr. Prickles without meaning to, what else might happen if he couldn't control Rodney? And how was he going to explain himself to Mrs. Root?

Chapter 11

Jack and Sally dumped their bags in the hallway and then ran out into the back garden. They climbed to the top of the climbing frame and sat with their legs dangling over the edge. They were soon joined by Max, who leapt across from the garage roof and into Jack's lap. He meowed loudly. Sally reached out and stroked him.

"Was Mrs. Root okay?"

Jack shrugged. He hadn't said anything on the way home. Mrs. Root hadn't believed him that he hadn't thrown the rubber and she'd written a letter for him to give to his mum. It was still in his bag.

"I wish I had a cat. He's ace."

Jack nodded in agreement. Max was more than just ace though. He wanted to tell Sally that he was sure Max was magical too. He glanced at Sally, and chewed his bottom lip while he tried to make up his mind. What if he told her about Max, but she just laughed at him?

Max stood up and arched his back. Jack tickled him between his ears and bent down to give him a proper cuddle. Max headbutted him.

"Hey! What was that for, Max?"

Max looked up at him and winked.

"Did he just do that?" exclaimed Sally

"Er...do what?" Jack struggled to keep his smile to himself.

"Winked. Your cat just winked."

"Oh, yes, he does that." Jack paused, then, before he lost his nerve, he added, "He does other stuff too, you know."

"What do you mean? What kind of stuff?"

Jack was convinced that being King Worm Jack was all down to Max. He'd been working it out.

He took a deep breath and then, in a rush, said, "Well, this might sound odd, but when I go to sleep, I have these dreams which aren't really dreams. It's like he magics me into my imagination, but way better. So last night, I was actually inside Mr. Prickles' head, and he has a room in there called 'Eyebrow Control'. His eyebrows really are caterpillars, and we set them free, and that's why he has no eyebrows anymore."

Jack was out of breath, he'd said it all so quickly before he lost his nerve. Sally was staring at him.

"You're making it up."

Jack shook his head. "I'm not, it's all true."

"How is that even possible?"

Jack shrugged, "Dunno. Just is."

Sally thought about it. "Did he really have caterpillar eyebrows?"

"He really did. And there are bogeymen *and* teardrop creatures." Jack stopped. He thought maybe he shouldn't say anything about being a worm. She probably wouldn't believe that.

"Can Max take us there now?"

Jack shook his head slowly. "I'm not sure if you can go. I think it's just me."

He didn't know if that was true, but he wasn't ready to let anyone else enter his special worm world. Not even Sally. Not just yet anyway.

She looked disappointed. "How does he make it happen, then?"

Max rubbed his nose on Jack's arm and Jack scratched him between his ears.

"Well, it's just before I go to sleep, after I've drawn something. He kind of headbutts my picture and then he sort of sends this zizz of light between us and...and...he winks."

Jack's cheeks were burning red with embarrassment. There was a silence while Sally thought for a bit.

"Can you make Mr. Prickles do something that proves you've been in his head?"

"Like what?"

Sally shrugged her shoulders. "I don't know. That's up to you."

Chapter 12

As Jack lay in bed with Max snuggled under the duvet with him, he wondered how he could prove to Sally that he was telling the truth.

He'd thought about taking her with him, so he'd drawn her standing next to him and Rodney in their wormsies, in front of the door with the 'Memories' sign on it. At the last minute, however, he'd rubbed her out. Sometimes, it could be awkward with three, and he wasn't ready to risk his friendship with Rodney.

Max was purring sleepily next to him. "What do you think, Max? What if I met Rodney and we tried out the memories room? We might find out something that only Mr. Prickles could know. Then I could prove to Sally that I've been in his brain." Jack waited, hoping that would be enough for Max's magic to work. Sure enough, there was a wink and a zizz and a tingle in his toes (that was new — maybe he was just excited?) and . . .

Rodney was waiting for him at the wooden door.

"Ready, Your Majesty?"

"Yep. Let's go!"

Jack unzipped his wormsie, and knocked as loudly as he could with the hedgehog doorknocker. In an instant, the hatch slid open. Barry the bogeyman glared out at them. The hatch slid sharply shut again and Barry's face disappeared. Surprised, Jack looked at Rodney, who shrugged, well, did a sort of Mexican wave down his body (worms can't shrug). Jack knocked again. The hatch opened.

"I can't let you in. Not after last time. Not after all that fuss in the eyebrow room."

"I'm really sorry about that," said Jack, "but the caterpillars looked so sad, and he doesn't need caterpillars as eyebrows. There must be something else he can have."

Barry regarded him for a moment, before grinning from one side of his blobby face to the other. "Well, actually young worm, you're right. The teardrops have found some lovely soft brushes to use instead." He frowned. "The problem is, though, that they're rather tickly and cause Mr. Prickles to twitch his face more than he should." He shook his head in a worried kind of way, and a few bogey bits dripped down the front of the door. Jack then realised that it hadn't been algae that he had seen on the door last time. He was glad he hadn't touched it.

"So, can we come in, then?" Rodney demanded.

Barry nodded at Jack. "He can, you can't. You caused all the trouble last time."

Rodney looked pleadingly at Jack. Jack stood up tall, adjusted his crown, and spoke with as much authority as he could manage, "Rodney is with me. I am King Worm Jack and I need Rodney by my side. He will be with me at all times, and I guarantee that he will cause no trouble." He suspected that wasn't a promise that would be easy to keep, but it was worth a try.

The hatch slid shut and, for a moment, Jack thought he had failed to convince Barry. Then it opened again and Barry squeaked, "Password!"

"Give us a clue?" asked Jack hopefully.

Barry grinned and spoke directly to Rodney with a mischievous twinkle in his eye. "What do hedgehogs like to eat? I'll give you another clue: they're small and slithery."

"Worms," grunted Rodney grumpily.

 *draw here*

The heavy wooden door swung open once more and Barry stood aside, grinning, to let them pass. Jack walked through the wooden door and straight across the room to the door with the sign, 'Memories', on it. He turned the handle. The door opened smoothly and quietly, and he and Rodney walked in.

Chapter 13

"Good evening, gentleworms. Pleased to meet you. My name's Molly. This way please," said a purple wobbly thing, holding a torch and pointing it in the direction she wanted them to go in. They were in a tiny cinema with just four seats and a giant screen.

"I'm afraid we're only showing one film tonight," sighed Molly sadly. "It's actually the only film we've been showing every night since the summer holidays."

Jack and Rodney sat down on the seats illuminated by Molly's torch. The seats were so comfy, it was like being cuddled by a huge, soft velvet teddy bear. Jack had a tonne of questions queuing up in his head, starting with, "Um, excuse me, no offence, but, um, what exactly are you?"

Molly wasn't at all offended. In fact, she seemed to find the question rather amusing. She started to laugh and was soon laughing so much that she wobbled just like a humongous jelly. "Oh, that's a good one!" she laughed. "I've not had a good giggle for weeks." She stopped laughing and whispered, "You see, this movie just makes me cry and it's on EVERY night." Molly shook her head sadly and purple tears dropped to the floor.

"I don't understand what's so funny." Jack frowned. "And I don't understand what part of the brain you are."

Molly looked surprised. "I'm the Memory Matron of course. It's my job to look after all the memories and to put them where they belong."

"I don't get it. What do you mean?" asked Jack.

 *draw here*

"Well, some memories need to go away into hibernation, some just need tucking up in bed for a bit, others need to come out to play, and some need to be nursed back to health, if they're feeling a bit peaky."

Jack's head was spinning as he tried to understand. "Do you mean that memories are actually like living things, that you look after?"

"Well, of course they are. What a silly question!"

"But don't I control my memories? Don't I decide what I want to remember?"

Molly smiled and shook her head. "Well, a lot of the time you do, but sometimes a memory just pops into your head from nowhere, doesn't it?"

Jack thought about it and realised that was true. Sometimes he thought about stuff that had happened and he had no idea why it had popped into his mind. Often it was something that had been really embarrassing, and it made him embarrassed all over again to remember it. He nodded.

"Well, when that happens, that's because a memory has taken control and plopped itself, unasked, onto that big screen over there. It's my job to take them back to where they need to be. Some of them think they're more important than they are, and they don't like being told what to do and where to go. That's when we get problems like the one we have now, for instance."

Molly stopped speaking and peered at Jack suspiciously. "You never said who you were."

"Oh, I'm King Worm Jack," said Jack, feeling very important, "and this is Chief Worm Rodney. We're on a special mission to make Mr. Prickles happy again."

"Oh, well in that case, I'm very pleased to meet you, King Worm Jack," said Molly, grinning, and held out her squelchy hand.

Chapter 14

Rodney nudged Jack and pointed at the big screen on the wall, which seemed to be showing a movie of a rabbit. Molly saw them looking and shielded her eyes from the screen.

"I can't bear to watch it anymore."

"What is it?" asked Jack curiously.

"Oh, this is the memory that just won't leave the screen. I've tried everything to get it off there, but it's hanging on so tightly, it won't budge." Molly sighed and tears started to drip down her cheeks and form a sticky purple puddle on the floor. Jack wondered whether the puddle would taste of blackcurrant jelly.

"It's just so sad, and I keep trying to get it off the screen but it either won't or can't, and you see, it's making Mr. Prickles so terribly miserable."

Jack stared at the screen, trying to work out what the image was. There was a little black and white rabbit in a hutch. It was sitting in the middle of a pile of vegetables: lettuces, green beans, peas and carrots.

Jack smiled; it was a very cute rabbit and he thought it must be very happy with all those vegetables. Though, perhaps it felt a bit crowded in its hutch: the piles of vegetables were bigger than the rabbit. He couldn't understand why such a happy looking rabbit could make Mr. Prickles so sad. He asked Molly.

Molly sighed, "Well, Mr. Prickles grows prize vegetables, and this year he was hoping to win the Tastiest Vegetable competition at the county show. But someone picked all his best vegetables and fed them to his rabbit."

Rodney and Jack looked at each other and back at the memory screen. Could that really make Mr. Prickles so unhappy? Jack asked Molly, "Is that why he's so miserable?"

"Oh yes," nodded Molly, her head flopping up and down. "Those vegetables are very important to him. That was a really mean thing to do."

"Oh," said Jack, still not really understanding how anyone could get so upset about a bunch of vegetables, even if it was mean of someone else to pick them all. "Well, it must be easy enough to just grow some more and cheer up a bit."

Rodney nodded in agreement. Molly looked at them both as if they were stupid. Jack wriggled uncomfortably in his seat. He hated that feeling of not knowing something that someone expected you to know.

Molly spoke slowly and loudly, like his dad spoke to his gran (who was deaf). "Those are his *prize* vegetables, that he was going to enter into the Tastiest Vegetable competition at the county show. It's not as easy as just growing some more. I think someone was jealous of him and deliberately sabotaged his chances of winning."

Jack chewed his lip, trying to work out what to do. "Well, how do we cheer him up, then?"

Molly sighed heavily, "The only way is to get this memory off the screen, but we can only do that if a more powerful, happy memory wants to take its place. Or, sometimes, a really brilliant new idea can knock the memory off."

Rodney cleared his throat loudly. "Um, Your Majesty, I've got a really brilliant new idea. We could actually help him win the Tastiest Vegetable competition."

"How?" asked Jack. "I thought he had no vegetables left. Anyway, Molly says it's not that easy to grow prize vegetables."

"It's easy for worms," grinned Rodney. "He's still got sprouts left, and I know just how to make them win."

"How do you know about his sprouts?" asked Molly.

"Oh," said Rodney, "we live underneath the allotment. We know all the vegetables."

Chapter 15

"So," asked Sally excitedly at school the next day, "how are you going to prove that Max is magical and you can get inside Mr. Prickles' brain?"

"Shhhh" whispered Jack, afraid that someone would hear her. "He has a rabbit."

Sally looked at him, like he had just said something extremely stupid. "So what?"

"Someone picked all the prize vegetables he was growing for the county vegetable competition and fed them to his rabbit and that's why he's miserable."

"Really?" Sally's eyes widened. "How do you know?"

Jack smiled, "Oh, Molly told me, when we went into the memory room."

Sally looked confused, "Who's Molly?"

"She looks after all the memories, and there's this one really stubborn memory of the rabbit which won't come off the memory screen, and that's why Mr. Prickles is so grumpy."

Sally looked at him in disbelief. "Really?"

Jack blushed. "It's true. Just wait and see. I'll prove it."

For once they were doing something interesting in class. It was art, and they were all drawing their favourite animals. Jack suddenly had a brilliant idea about how he could prove to Sally that he had been inside Mr. Prickles' brain. Soon, he was concentrating really hard. In fact, he was concentrating so hard, he didn't notice Mr. Prickles standing over him.

"Glad to see you're concentrating today, Jack."

He actually said it in a friendly voice, but his voice made Jack jump. Jack began to think that his brilliant idea wasn't so brilliant after all, so he quickly slammed his hand over his piece of paper to hide his drawing.

Mr. Prickles' eyebrows were twitching. They were a definite improvement on the caterpillar eyebrows, Jack thought.

"What don't you want me to see, Jack?"

"Oh, it's j...just I haven't f... finished it yet, Mr. Prickles," spluttered Jack. "I don't want you to see it until I've f...finished."

"Okay, then. Very secretive. It must be a masterpiece you're creating."

Mr. Prickles turned away and Jack relaxed his hand. He didn't expect Mr. Prickles to spin back round and snatch up his drawing.

Jack watched in horror as Mr. Prickles stared at his picture, his eyes growing wider every second. But when Mr. Prickles spoke, his voice was soft and trembling, not at all like his usual shouty voice.

"That's a very good drawing of a rabbit. Is it your rabbit?"

Jack bit his lip. This was his chance to prove to Sally that he was telling the truth about getting into Mr. Prickles' brain, but Mr. Prickles was making him nervous. He didn't want to say anything now. "Um, no, it's just a...a...random rabbit."

Mr. Prickles appeared to study the picture with care.

"It appears to have a lot of vegetables to eat."

Jack swallowed down the big lump of saliva that was stuck in his throat.

Mr. Prickles was looking straight at Jack now. Jack shut his eyes, anticipating the shout that was clearly going to come out of Mr. Prickles' mouth. Instead, Mr. Prickles bent down and spoke softly into Jack's ear, "Come and see me at break time." Then he walked back to his desk, taking Jack's unfinished drawing with him.

Chapter 16

Jack could feel butterflies in his tummy and wondered if they were special real tummy butterflies. He'd like to tell them to go away if he could, because they were making him feel a bit sick.

What was Mr. Prickles going to say to him at break time? He glanced at Sally, and she shook her head at him, as if to say, "You're in BIG trouble."

At break time, when everyone else went out, Jack stayed behind, and Sally hovered behind him, pretending to tie up her shoelaces. Mr. Prickles strode over, pulled out a chair and sat down next to him, placing Jack's drawing on the table in front of them.

He stabbed the picture with his index finger, "So, tell me about this picture."

"I...I don't know what you mean," stammered Jack. He wished Sally hadn't asked him to prove anything. He didn't want to do this anymore. He glanced at Sally, who was hopping from one foot to another, with a grin floating across her face.

"Does it look like your rabbit, Mr. Prickles?" asked Sally. "Does it? I bet it does! Jack's brilliant at drawing!"

Mr. Prickles turned slowly to look at Sally. He narrowed his eyes. "I'm struggling to understand why Jack would be able to draw such an accurate picture, not only of my rabbit, but of its hutch, and even down to the vegetables it eats. And now, Sally, I'm wondering what you have to do with this."

He raised his eyebrows. Jack's heart was now thumping so hard, it was like he could feel the rabbit's feet pummelling against his chest, trying to run away.

Sally bit her fingernail, "I don't have anything to do with it, Mr. Prickles. I just, well, I liked Jack's picture and just thought that maybe you had a rabbit, too."

"Really?"

Sally nodded.

"I suppose you also thought that I might have some prize-winning vegetables? Vegetables that someone picked and fed to my rabbit." He paused. "I don't suppose you two know anything about that?"

With a sudden stab of horror, Jack realised that Mr. Prickles might think he and Sally had been responsible for destroying his prize vegetables.

"It wasn't us! We didn't do it." Jack blurted out.

"Get out."

"But..."

"Please go out to the playground. Now."

"Mr. Pri..." Sally started to say, but Jack shook his head violently at her, to stop her saying anything else that would make it worse. They reached the classroom door and just before they left, Jack turned round to look at Mr. Prickles.

He was sitting where they had left him, holding Jack's picture. A tear was trickling down his face.

Chapter 17

Sally came home with Jack after school to plan what they were going to do next about Mr. Prickles. Mum let them have a piece of cake each in the kitchen and he and Sally wolfed it down, so that they could get on with their planning. Seb and mum were sitting at the table with them.

"What's the rush, you two?" asked mum.

Seb smirked at them, "They fancy each other. They want to tell each other how much they love each other and they're too embarrassed in front of us."

Jack glared at Seb. "Do not. Don't talk rubbish."

Max swiped his paw at Scarlet, who slunk away between Seb's legs.

"Hey, get your disgusting cat away from my dog!"

"*He's* not disgusting. *You're* disgusting!"

"Boys! Stop it!"

Seb was still smirking at Jack. Jack looked at Sally, who was bright red and concentrating really hard on picking up every last crumb of cake on her plate.

"Oh, by the way, I found this lying around." Seb waved an envelope in front of Jack and handed it to their mum.

"What's this, Seb?"

Jack choked on a mouthful of cake as he recognised the letter Mrs. Root had given him to give to his mum.

Seb smirked. "I think it's a letter from Jack's school."

Their mum frowned as she opened the envelope and pulled a sheet of paper out. Her expression darkened as she read the letter.

"C'mon, Sally." Jack slipped off his stool and grabbed Sally's arm, intending to creep quietly out of the kitchen.

"Where do you think you're going?"

"Just upstairs," mumbled Jack.

His mum glared at him. "How long have you had this letter?"

Jack shrugged.

"Don't shrug at me." His mum's voice was getting louder. She slammed the letter down on the table. "Why didn't you tell me about this?"

Seb, who must have read the letter over his mum's shoulder, whistled in amazement. "You threw a rubber at Mr. Prickles?"

"He didn't! It's not true!" exclaimed Sally.

Jack's mum raised her eyebrows, "Thank you Sally, but I don't think we need your comments right now."

Sally bit her lip and played with the crumbs on her plate, blushing furiously.

"Well, Jack? What do you have to say?"

"Sally's right. I didn't do anything. Well, not in the classroom anyway. Nothing that I meant to do. I mean it was Rodney, not me. And he couldn't have known that would happen."

His mum rubbed her hand over her forehead. "I have no idea what you're talking about. I'm calling Sally's parents so they can pick her up and you can go straight to your room. NOW."

Sally shrank into her seat, trying to be as invisible as possible. Jack ran out of the kitchen, tears streaming down his face.

"I hate you, Seb!" he yelled as he ran upstairs.

Chapter 18

Jack shuffled into the classroom the next morning, with his head down. He didn't want to talk to anyone, especially not Sally. His mum had been SO embarrassing last night, making Sally go home and sending him to his bedroom. And it was all Seb's fault.

"Hey, Jack!" Sally whispered as she nudged his arm. "You okay?"

Jack nodded but said nothing.

"Your brother's really mean."

"I know. You're lucky you don't have a brother," he muttered.

"Quiet, please!"

They sat down and Jack groaned. There on the desk in front of every child was a maths worksheet.

"Right. I want quiet NOW!" shouted Mr. Prickles.

"An hour of maths and then we're going to start thinking about the county creative writing competition."

"Yes!" whispered Sally under her breath.

"No," groaned Jack at the same time.

"Three years ago, we had a winner from this very class," Mr. Prickles paused and gazed around the classroom, before his eyes settled on Jack. "Seb Wrigglesworth won, isn't that right, Jack?"

Jack nodded glumly.

"Well, maybe this will be our winning year again. But first, it's time for fractions. You have an hour. Let's see how much you can remember."

One very long hour later and Jack had only managed half the questions and he wasn't even sure they were right. He peered over at Sally's worksheet. She'd finished and noticed him looking.

"Do you want some help?" she whispered.

Jack nodded. Sally reached over to pull his worksheet towards her.

"WHAT are you two talking about? Would you care to share it with the rest of us?"

Jack shook his head.

Mr. Prickles raised his eyebrows, "I'm waiting, Jack."

Jack squirmed uncomfortably in his seat.

"Come on, spit it out."

Jack glanced at Sally.

"Don't check with Sally. You don't need her approval, you need mine."

Some of the class started to snigger. Jack could feel his cheeks burning.

"Um, I...I just, um, ..."

"Right, you can finish this off, while the rest of the class go out for break."

More of the class sniggered. Jack's chest felt tight, resentment building up inside him.

"Then after break, let's see if you can write a story as good as your brother's, shall we?"

Jack felt tears bubbling up at the back of his eyes.

"I want to see you putting some effort in, Jack. I know you can do better than this."

The tears started to escape down Jack's face, and he wiped some away with his sleeve.

"If you spent less time daydreaming and chatting to your best friend," Mr. Prickles glared at Sally, "and more time concentrating, you would be doing much better in my class."

Something inside Jack snapped. He was sick of worksheets. He was sick of Mr. Prickles being mean and horrible. He was sick of Seb and, worst of all, he was sick of everyone thinking he was useless. He jumped up from the table and yelled, "I WISH I WAS A WORM!" and then he ran out of the classroom and slammed the door.

He ran down the corridor and out into the playground, and kept on running until he reached the school gate. He sank down to the ground, with his back against the gate and pulled his knees into his chest. He buried his head in his hands, so no one could see him crying. He was going to be in BIG trouble.

Chapter 19

Actually, he didn't get into as much trouble as he thought he would. Mrs. Root came out and found him and they went back into her office, and she got Mr. Prickles to come in, too.

He and Mr. Prickles had to apologise to each other, which was a bit awkward, especially as it was like Mr. Prickles was in trouble as well. He even told Jack that he liked him and just wanted him to try harder, because he knew he could do better. He didn't say anything about Jack being useless. Jack had to promise never to run out of school again, and that was it.

The rest of the day went quite quickly, though some of his class kept whispering, "I wish I was a worm," and sniggering whenever they were near him. Jack tried to ignore them. The first time someone said it, Sally had leaned over and whispered to him, "I wish I was a worm, too. They're really cool."

Jack knew that she was just being nice to him, but what if he could get her to come with him on his adventures? Then she'd *really* know how cool worms were. He decided he would ask Max tonight and see if they could make it happen.

His mum was quiet when she picked him up after school. When they got home and they'd had a snack, she made him sit next to her on the sofa. Max jumped up onto his lap, and snuggled in quietly, for once.

"I had a phonecall from school today."

Jack's heart sank. He thought she would never have to know.

"Do you want to tell me what happened?"

Jack shrugged. "Dunno really."

His mum waited, and then, when he said nothing, she said, "Well, something must have happened to make you run out of school in the middle of a lesson."

Jack sighed. "Mr. Prickles was horrible, and he's always being horrible, and it's the creative writing competition and I'm useless at writing and Seb won it before, and Mr. Prickles wants someone to win it this year and it'll never be me and...and...."

"Hey, Jack," his mum put her arm round him and pulled him close. "Where's all this come from?"

Jack said nothing. His mum squeezed him tight in against her. "You're not useless, Jack. Wherever did you get that idea from?"

"You're always going on about how amazing Seb is. Everyone thinks he's brilliant at everything. Even Mr. Prickles does."

"Oh, Jack. What am I going to do with you?"

Jack shrugged.

"I don't think you're useless. You're my beautiful, creative, funny little boy."

Jack squirmed away. "Mu-um, boys aren't beautiful," he complained, though he was trying not to smile.

"Well, you are. And who's the artist in this house? Hey?"

"Me?" asked Jack, doubtfully.

"Yes, you. Why don't you do a cartoon strip or something for that writing competition?"

That was actually quite a good idea. "Maybe," Jack muttered.

"And I've been talking to some of the other mums, and it seems you're right; Mr. Prickles has not quite been himself recently. Apparently, he's having a tough time at home at the moment. It's not an excuse, but it does explain why he's being grumpy with you."

"I know," Jack nodded. He felt his mum staring at him.

"What do you know?"

"Something happened to his prize vegetables. I'm going to put it right and then he can cheer up and be nice again. Then you won't think he's being horrible just because of me."

His mum looked confused. "Why would I think that?"

"Because you said so. You said I must be winding him up. And I'm not."

"Oh, Jack!" His mum pulled away from him and tried to look him in the face, but Jack refused to look up at her.

"Listen, *if* I said that, I'm sorry, but you need to let him sort his own problems out. I'm not sure what vegetables have to do with it, but I do know it's not something you can solve. Okay?"

"S'ppose," muttered Jack.

"Right, well, let's have no more feeling useless and being miserable. Deal?"

Jack nodded. "Can I go now?" Without waiting for an answer, he ran upstairs, shut his door and grabbed his sketchpad from under his pillow. He *could* sort out Mr. Prickles' problems and he was going to prove it, but it was time to ask for Sally's help. He drew her standing in between himself and Rodney, and grinned. She was going to be amazed!

Chapter 20

Jack was back in the familiar surroundings of Mr. Prickles' brain, standing in front of the door with the hedgehog doorknocker. Next to him was Rodney, and next to him was Sally. Rodney was staring at Sally. Sally was staring at everything.

"Oh, it worked then," said Jack. Rodney and Sally both turned to stare at him.

"Hey? What?" spluttered Sally.

"Your Majesty, who is this worm with the funny hair?"

It was true, Jack thought, Sally's curly blonde hair did look a bit funny on top of a worm head. He reached forward and undid her wormsie for her. She started waving her hands about in amazement, which made her look even more weird.

"Your Majesty, do you actually know this worm?"

Jack nodded. "Yes, she's a friend of mine."

Rodney looked a bit upset. "Oh, I see. Oh well then, if you don't need me anymore, I'll just, um, go then and leave you to it."

Rodney didn't move though. He stayed where he was, looking glumly at the floor. Sally was now excitedly rushing around the tiny space, touching everything and exclaiming in wonder.

"This is amazing! Are we really inside Mr. Prickles' head? This is SO cool. And did he just call you, 'Your Majesty'?"

Jack smiled proudly and touched his crown. "Yep, I'm King Worm Jack."

"That's epic! I get it now! I get why you want to be a worm!"

Rodney started to shuffle away slowly.

"Hey Rodney! Don't go. I need you. Please come back."

Rodney came back in one happy skid. "Right here, Your Majesty." He grinned at Jack and then scowled at Sally.

"Allow me to introduce you two: Chief Worm Rodney and Chief, um, Thinker, Sally."

Rodney nodded briefly to Sally. Sally stuck out her hand and grabbed Rodney's to give it a shake.

"Chief Worm? How cool. What did you call me, Jack?"

"Chief Thinker."

"Epic. Thanks. Are we really worms?"

Rodney nudged Jack and whispered, "Are you sure she's Chief Thinker? She seems a bit dim to me, if she doesn't know that she's a worm."

Before Jack could answer, the door swung open and Barry squeaked, "Are you going to stand there all day or are you coming in?"

"Coming in," answered Jack, but as he stepped through the doorway, Barry stopped him with a glistening, gloopy hand.

"New rules. You need a pass, especially since you've brought a friend. We can't have his brain overrun with worms who don't belong. It's an hour's pass." Barry stuck a badge shaped bogey on Jack's chest.

Sally wrinkled her nose in disgust as Barry stuck a dripping bogey badge on her too.

"What happens if we're longer than an hour?" asked Jack.

"We come in and get you." Barry grinned and winked at Jack. "And we bring our bogey guns."

Rodney shivered at the memory and started brushing himself down with his hands, as if he were already covered in snot.

"Come on, no time to lose." Jack led them into the hallway with doors and rushed straight over to the door that said, 'Brainworks.' Sally stood for so long gazing at the different doors that Rodney had to drag her over with him. He looked at Jack, shaking his head and whispering, "She's Chief Thinker? No way."

Jack heaved the 'Brainworks' door open and they found themselves in another small hallway with three doors, each with a sign on it. Jack read the signs out loud, "'Ideas Room,' 'Command Centre,' 'Feelings.'" He scratched his head, unsure which to open.

"I say we try the Command Centre," said Rodney. "We can command him to enter that vegetable competition."

"What do you mean?" asked Sally.

"Rodney reckons that he can get Mr. Prickles' sprouts to win the Tastiest Vegetable competition. We think that will cheer him up."

Rodney bounced up and down excitedly. "Come on! What are you waiting for?"

Jack looked at Sally. She was shaking her head. "No, it's always better if you have the idea yourself instead of someone telling you to do something."

True, thought Jack. He much preferred doing his own ideas than being made to do something that someone else wanted him to do.

Sally carried on, "so, we should go into the Ideas Room and then put an idea into his head that he should enter the competition, then that idea can go into the Command Centre and then he'll feel happy because he'll think he thought of it all by himself."

Jack nodded slowly. That made sense to him. He glanced at Rodney to see if he agreed, but Rodney was being all sulky and refusing to look at him. Jack sighed. He hadn't thought Rodney was going to be such hard work.

Jack opened the door to the Ideas Room, and they all slipped inside.

Chapter 21

The Ideas Room looked a bit like a really cool soft play area. There were rope swings, beanbags, climbing walls, mini trampolines, a sofa, and a desk with one swivel chair. On the wall next to the desk there were two letterboxes with signs above. The signs were, 'Approved Ideas,' and 'Rejected Ideas.'

It was quite dark in the room, but it was easy to see that there were things playing on all the equipment and sitting on the beanbags, because they were glowing, like the glow-in-the dark wrist things you get at parties. They were chatting and shouting and doing backflips and running and bouncing off the walls. All except one, who was smaller than the rest. He was sitting in the swivel chair by the desk, watching them all.

Rodney had already wriggled off to play on the trampoline, so Sally and Jack went over to the small creature in the chair. He looked a bit like the dangly thing at the back of your throat. They all did. He didn't look pleased to see them. Jack cleared his throat and did his best King voice.

"Excuse me, we're here to help Mr. Prickles with an idea."

The small creature looked surprised and said nothing. Jack tried to explain.

"You see, Mr. Prickles needs to enter the Tastiest Vegetable competition, but he doesn't know that he needs to. Not yet, anyway."

The creature looked more interested and answered in a sing-song voice, "Well, this *is* the ideas room, so you're in the right place."

Sally peered at him and asked, "What are you?"

Jack thought that was a bit rude, but the creature didn't seem to think so. He smiled, "I'm the little voice at the back of your head." He gestured to all the other creatures, "and these are the other voices in your head that tell you what you should do."

Jack thought about his head. It didn't make any sense.

"But I don't have any voices in my head, that's just me."

The little voice smiled and tapped his head in a knowing kind of way. "Oh, well they all sound the same, apart from me, so most people can't tell them apart."

Sally was wriggling around excitedly. "I get it! You mean, when I'm thinking of ideas, even though I can just hear my own voice in my head, it's like there are lots of voices all speaking in my voice, giving me their ideas."

The little voice grinned, "That's exactly it!"

 draw here

Jack frowned, not sure he liked the idea of creatures in his head that pretended to be his own voice. "So, what do you do, then?"

The little voice grinned again and said in a very smug voice, "Well, I'm the little voice at the back of your head that says things like, 'Are you sure about that?' or 'You can't do that!' or, 'That's not a very good idea!' By the way, my name's Jeff."

Jack didn't like him. He didn't like the annoying voice at the back of his own head that said exactly those things. Sally seemed quite impressed, though.

"That's epic! So, you can give Mr. Prickles the idea about the sprouts, then?"

"Oh no." Jeff shook his head. "I can only take ideas from the voices, not from *worms*. And I might choose to reject the idea anyway." His eyes sparkled at them. "Anyway, as you can see," he gestured around them, "the voices are a little distracted at the moment."

Chapter 22

They turned around and saw that Rodney had organised the voices into two teams and was playing a game of headers (like volleyball, but you used your head, not your hands). There was no way they would be able to get the voices' attention: they were having far too much fun.

Jack jumped onto the desk and yelled, "PLEASE LISTEN TO ME! WE NEED YOUR HELP!"

Nothing happened. He glanced at Jeff, who was grinning and swinging himself round and round in his swivel chair.

Jack glared in Rodney's direction, but he was too busy cheering for his team to notice. He tried again, "THIS IS AN EMERGENCY! MR. PRICKLES NEEDS YOUR HELP!"

The room fell silent. Sally was looking up admiringly at Jack. "You're such an epic King Worm," she whispered. Jack blushed with pride. He glanced over at Jeff, who scowled at him.

The voices came and sat down on the beanbags and sofa, and Rodney shuffled sheepishly over to the desk Jack was standing on. He whispered up to Jack, "I was just getting to know them, that's all. And my team was winning; we'd nearly finished the game."

Jack whispered back, "It's fine. Don't worry about it." He adjusted his crown, cleared his throat and was about to speak when the desk he was standing on shook violently and overturned.

Luckily, he just managed to roll out of the way before the table fell on top of him and split him into two. Being a worm could be dangerous. Jeff grinned at him, from where he was now standing, right next to the overturned desk.

"Oops." Jeff smiled again. "It always was a bit wobbly."

Jack stared at him suspiciously.

Jeff addressed the voices, "It seems Mr. Prickles has a problem that needs solving and these...these *worms* would like your help." Jeff spat out the word, 'worms' like it was something really disgusting, like eating your own bogies.

Jack felt a bit put out. He wasn't *just* a worm. He was King Worm Jack. He stood up tall, checked his crown wasn't wonky after his fall, and spoke. "Mr. Prickles is miserable, because someone destroyed all his prize vegetables, but we can help him. He just needs to have the idea that he could enter his sprouts for the Tastiest Vegetable competition. Can one of you suggest it for us?"

 draw here

There was silence and a stillness in the room, and then chaos broke out. The voices leapt up and started doing backflips and leapfrogging over each other, all the time chatting, so that the room was filled with noise.

Jack, Rodney and Sally looked at each other in confusion. Jeff came over and explained, "This is how they think. They'll quieten down soon and suggest their ideas. If you're lucky, they'll suggest yours, too." He grinned slyly, "and then I'll probably reject it."

Jeff went back to his swivel chair, whistling cheerfully. Jack, Sally and Rodney sank down onto the sofa and waited. Jack felt deflated, like an empty balloon.

Jeff had been right: the voices did settle down and one of them did suggest the sprout idea and Jeff did reject it. In fact, all Jeff ever seemed to say was, "Oh that wouldn't work," or "That's a stupid idea."

They were all getting bored, even Jeff looked bored saying no to everything. Worse than that, Jack knew their hour was nearly up, and he was feeling sleepy, which was always a sign that he was going to wake up in bed soon. He nudged Sally, "Think of something. You're Chief Thinker. We need your help."

"Yeah, *think* of something," added Rodney.

Sally frowned her Chief Thinker's frown and then she wandered over to Jeff and whispered into his ear. He shook his head fiercely at first, but she whispered something else, and he gave a grudging smile and nodded.

He scribbled something down on a piece of paper, stamped it and posted it through the 'Approved Ideas' letterbox. Then Sally whispered to him again and he scribbled something else, stamped that too and posted it through the same letterbox.

The voices all cheered, "Hurray!" Jeff stood up and, to Jack's astonishment, he did a little victory dance and then a double cartwheel. The voices all cheered again, "Hurray for Jeff!"

"What did you say to him?" Jack asked Sally in amazement.

"Oh, I just said that I bet it feels amazing when you're the one that approves the ideas. It must be like you're the one in charge of all the brilliant stuff that Mr. Prickles does. I said I wished I could do what he does. Then I asked him to show me what would happen if he did approve our idea. It worked." Sally grinned triumphantly.

"What was the second idea you asked him to approve?" asked Rodney suspiciously.

"Oh, just something," Sally was beaming. "You'll see."

Chapter 23

When Jack walked into the classroom the next day, he almost turned round and walked right out again. He thought he'd gone into the wrong classroom. Mr. Prickles was whistling, happily. On each table was a treasure map, a set of cards, with the word, "Clues" written on the top card, and a bag of marshmallows.

"Class, keep your coats on! We are having an outdoor learning day today."

"Where are we going?"

"Can we make a fire?"

"Are we out *all* day?"

"I didn't bring a packed lunch."

"I didn't ask my mum."

Jack nudged Sally, "What's going on?"

Sally smirked at him, "Well, Jeff approved two ideas. Remember?"

"This was *your* idea?"

"Yep!"

"Wow! You're brilliant!"

"Thanks," said Sally, blushing.

"Settle down, everyone! You don't need packed lunches and you don't need permission from your parents, because we'll be in the school grounds. I've organised a treasure trail for you. And yes, we can make fires because we'll be toasting marshmallows. You need to bring your drawing books and your literacy books. Off we go!"

Jack wished every day could be like this. He'd won a prize for the most inventive mud sculpture (it was a bogeyman fighting a worm); they'd raced around the treasure trail and Jack realised he knew loads of stuff about plants and insects, so his team had won the treasure trail as well.

They'd even found a hedgehog, so everyone had a go at drawing it, even Mr. Prickles. Then the class made it a special hibernation hedgehog den, because Mr. Prickles said something must have happened to its home. He said it should be hibernating already, and it needed their help. He seemed to know a lot about hedgehogs.

 *draw here*

And finally, they were sitting around a fire, toasting marshmallows, when Mr. Prickles said, "I'd like everyone to share a wish with the rest of us; something that you really wish you could make happen."

Some of his class said stuff like, "I wish I could fly," or "I wish we could do this every day." Jack wished both of those things too, but what he said was, "I wish that I loved sprouts." He didn't really, but he wanted to make Mr. Prickles say something about the competition, to see if their plan had really worked.

Mr. Prickles stared at him curiously, and then said, "Well, Jack, I might be able to help you with that, because I am going to grow the tastiest sprouts that you have ever eaten."

"How do you know you are, Mr. Prickles?" asked Sally.

He grinned at them, "A little voice told me that this is going to be my best year yet for sprouts. I shall be entering them into the Tastiest Vegetable competition at the county show, and we'll see if I'm right."

"I bet you win, Mr. Prickles!" Jack could barely contain his excitement. Their plan was working, Mr. Prickles was already happier, and he'd just had the best day ever at school. Brilliant!

Chapter 24

Jack invited Sally over to his house after school to celebrate their amazing day. They went straight into the garden and climbed on to the top of the climbing frame where they thought they could chat without being overheard. No such luck. As soon as they'd sat down, Jack's brother and his friend, Tom, came out into the garden.

"So, your girlfriend's here again, then?" shouted Seb. Tom laughed.

"She's not my girlfriend; she's my friend." Jack glared at his brother.

"Oh, so she's not a girl?" Seb smirked. Tom laughed again.

Sally jumped down and put her hands on her hips, "I *am* a girl and I *am* his friend, and *you're* an idiot."

"Oooo!" said Seb.

"Touchy," said Tom.

Max came out from behind the garage and yowled at Seb. Scarlet, who'd been running around in circles, stopped next to Seb and barked at Max.

"I bet your mangy cat can't do tricks."

"Of course he can," replied Jack, wondering what sort of tricks Seb meant.

"Watch this! Come on, Scarlet, jump! Good girl! And again! Good girl."

Scarlet was standing on her hind legs and jumping up for a treat.

"That's rubbish," said Sally, "Max can do something much better than that."

"Oh really?" asked Seb, "Like what?"

"We're not showing you," said Jack, with a warning look at Sally.

"That's because he can't do anything. He's just a cat. I'm entering Scarlet into the Best Pet Trick competition at the county show next weekend." Seb looked very pleased with himself. Tom looked impressed too.

"I bet Max could beat Scarlet," said Sally, and stuck her tongue out at Seb.

"Really? Right then," he grinned, "I dare you to enter him, Jack. I'd like to see that, wouldn't you, Tom?" Seb and Tom both laughed so hard they started rolling around on the ground. Pretend laughter, Jack thought. Nobody laughed that much in real life.

Max rubbed himself against Sally's legs and meowed. Jack jumped down from the climbing frame. He had to get Sally inside quickly, before she said anything else. He grabbed her arm, and they ran inside and up to his bedroom, followed by Max.

Jack plonked himself onto the floor and Max leapt into his lap.

"Now, look what you've done! I'll *have* to enter the competition now, but Max can't do any tricks," said Jack, stroking Max's back. He purred and rubbed his nose on Jack's other hand.

"He's an epic cat. I bet he can do tricks, can't you, Max?"

Max meowed.

Jack scratched Max behind his ears, "I'm really not sure he can."

"Of course he can. He's magic! He'll do the best tricks ever, you'll see."

Jack shrugged. It was okay for Sally. She wasn't the one who'd have to take Max to the show and stand in front of everyone waiting for him to do some kind of trick. He wished she hadn't said anything. Max was brilliant, but he wouldn't beat Seb's dog in the Best Pet Trick competition. He felt slightly sick at the thought.

The doorbell shrilled through the house.

"That'll be my mum. See you tonight in wormland!" grinned Sally as she leapt off the bed and ran downstairs.

Chapter 25

They were zooming down a tunnel, zipped up into their wormsies, Rodney in the lead, Jack and Sally hurtling along behind him. It was awesome! Jack wondered what age you had to be to start training for the Olympics bobsleigh team. He thought he might find out when he was back home.

They were on their way to Mr. Prickles' allotment, where Rodney said he had a surprise for them both. Mr. Prickles' brain would just have to wait for another time.

Rodney skidded to a stop. Jack crashed straight into him. Sally somersaulted over the top of them both and landed in a heap in front of Rodney.

Rodney chuckled, "You both need to practise more."

Rodney wriggled upright and knocked on the door in front of them. A worm, wearing protective goggles and holding a tiny leaf, opened the door just a fraction and then, seeing Jack, swung it right open.

"Oh, King Worm Jack! How wonderful to see you! We've been really looking after Mr. Prickles' sprouts. I think they're going to be the stars of the show. Come in! Come in!" and he ushered them all through the door.

Jack raised his eyebrows at Sally, and she pulled a confused face back at him. They followed the worm inside and stopped when they saw what was in front of them.

"Ta da!" said Rodney triumphantly.

Jack and Sally looked at him and said nothing, speechless.

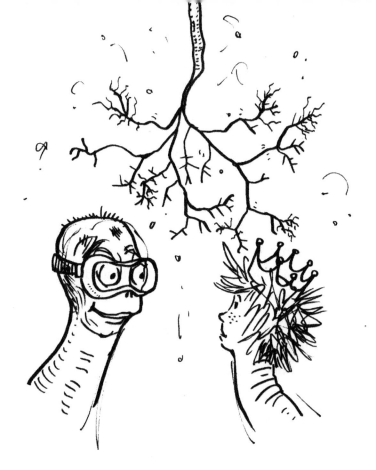

"Ta da!" Rodney said again.

"Um," said Jack.

"Er," said Sally.

"Aren't you impressed?" demanded Rodney.

It *was* impressive, but Jack had no idea what was going on. In front of them, were rows of roots, dangling down from the ceiling. Each set of roots had at least six worms stroking and tickling them with tiny leaves. Every time they were tickled, the roots squirmed and shook, which sent flakes of mud flying everywhere. That explained the protective goggles.

"Where are we?" asked Jack.

"In the sprout nursery, of course!"

On a platform to their right was a worm band, playing lullaby music on flutes made out of twigs. Then at intervals along the floor, Jack could see tunnels, and every now and then, a worm in a hard hat would appear.

Rodney couldn't stay sulky for long. He rushed over to the first set of roots. "Look at this one. Beautiful, isn't she?"

"Um, I suppose so," said Jack.

"Oh, you should have seen them before we got to work. Some of them were badly swollen and in such pain. Too much water, you see. So we dug some tunnels to drain away the water. We're just reinforcing the tunnels now, to make sure they don't collapse before the competition."

Sally was wandering between the roots, stroking them, "So, do they like this, then?"

"Of course they do! Can't you tell?"

"Not really, Rodney, no."

Rodney turned to Jack and whispered to him, "I don't think you should have made her Chief Thinker. She's not very good at thinking."

Jack said nothing. Rodney spoke loudly and clearly to Sally, like he was explaining something to someone very young or very stupid. "The tickling gives them exercise, the stroking makes them happy, the music makes them relax. Can't you hear them humming?"

Jack strained his ears but couldn't hear any humming. Obviously Sally couldn't either, because she was shaking her head.

"So, what do you think?" Rodney beamed at Jack.

"It's great," said Jack, uncertainly.

"He'll definitely win the Tastiest Vegetable competition now!" Rodney exclaimed.

"Are you sure?" asked Sally.

Rodney rolled his eyes at Jack. "Of course."

Chapter 26

School wasn't so bad the next day. They were working on their creative writing entries for the competition and Jack had been doing a cartoon strip, like his mum suggested. He'd called it, "The Best Sprouts Ever" and drawn a cartoon strip story of himself, Rodney and Sally working as secret worm gardeners, helping Mr. Prickles win the prize.

At lunchtime, Sally dragged Jack out of the lunch queue and pushed him into the cloakroom, next to their classroom.

"What are you doing?" hissed Jack, annoyed that he was missing lunch. It was roast day, and he'd been looking forward to it.

"Didn't you see him?" whispered Sally.

"See who?"

"Mr. Prickles, of course." Sally was bending down, peering into the classroom. "Come on, get down. We'll have to crawl in, in case anyone can see us through the windows."

Jack dropped to his hands and knees. "What are you talking about?"

"Mr. Prickles was writing a card when we were doing our stories. I saw him. He shut it away in his drawer and then he looked all sad." Sally pushed the classroom door open and started to crawl in.

"So what?"

"So, if he's sad, then our sprout plan might not work."

"Why not?"

"Because he might be sad about something else. We have to find out what he was writing that made him sad."

"But how are we going to do that?" asked Jack, not really wanting to hear Sally's answer.

"We have to search in his desk, of course and find the card."

Jack's mouth was dry with nerves. He didn't want to get into trouble again. "No, we can't do that. What if he finds us?"

"He won't. He's having lunch. Come on!"

Sally had crawled across the floor and was beckoning to him from under Mr. Prickles' desk.

Jack slithered across the floor to join her, thinking that now would be a really good time to be a worm.

"Right, I'll take this drawer," said Sally, "you take that one." Jack knelt in front of the right-hand drawer, Sally knelt in front of the left one. He hesitated. "Are you really sure we should be doing this?"

"Yes! We're not doing anything wrong. We're helping him!"

They pulled the drawers open and started rummaging through them. If he wasn't so scared about getting caught, Jack might have let himself get more distracted by the contents of his drawer: chewing gum, mints, a diary, pens, pencils, sticky notes, a cuddly hedgehog, a Twix. Jack was starving. He wondered if Mr. Prickles would notice if the Twix was gone.

"Found it!" shouted Sally, triumphantly.

Jack realised he had let himself get distracted after all.

"The envelope is addressed to Judy Prickles."

"I bet that's his wife!" exclaimed Jack.

"Epic. Let's take it and go."

Jack looked at her in horror. "We can't just take it. It's private. What are we going to do with it anyway?"

Sally looked at him as if he was stupid, "Open it and read it, of course, to find clues."

Jack bit his lip, and while he was still thinking, Sally slipped the card out of the envelope.

"Look! It's a soppy one." She showed him the front that had an embroidered loveheart made out of flowers, and then she giggled, opened it and read it out to him.

"Dear Judy, I'm so sorry for everything. I'm sorry for being grumpy. Of course I love you more than I love my vegetables. Please come home. I don't care about the stupid vegetables. I love you so much. Yours as always, Prickly. Kiss kiss kiss."

Chapter 27

Jack and Sally took the card and envelope with them and hid behind the coats in the cloakroom.

Sally was giggling again. "He called himself Prickly!"

But Jack was thinking about the vegetables. "Do you think *she* did it?"

"Did what?" asked Sally, still laughing.

"Picked all his vegetables and fed them to his rabbit."

"Probably. She must have been really cross with him. I wonder what he did to annoy her?"

"I dunno. But we need her to come back to him. Just winning the sprout competition won't be enough to cheer him up."

"Well, we better help him persuade her," said Sally, "because that card's rubbish. I think we need to add a bit more to it and invite her to come to the county vegetable competition. Then she'll see him winning, she'll be relieved she left him some sprouts, so she won't feel bad about ruining all the other vegetables *and* she'll be proud of him. Then they'll be friends again. Then she'll come home, and Mr. Prickles will be happy and nice again. It's a perfect plan!"

Jack wasn't sure. What if his wife knew he hadn't written the extra things in the card? Wouldn't that make it worse? But Sally was already writing.

"Shush!" she glared at him when he tried to stop her. "He'll never win her back with what he wrote. Trust me. This will work."

She read it out to Jack when she'd finished, and then declared it ready to be posted. They read it through one last time.

♡ ♡ ♡ ♡ ♡ ♡ ♡ ♡ ♡ ♡ ♡ ♡ ♡ ♡ ♡

You are the best
You make me laugh so much that sometimes my face hurts
You make me feel as safe as a caterpillar wrapped in a cocoon
You are as funny as the best joke book ever written
I love you a million, trillion, zillion times and to the moon and back
You're the most epic super woman in the whole universe.
You are the best ever.
Ps Please come and see my sprouts at the gala because they are really tasty and I really really want you to be proud of me.
Lots of love, your lovely husband, who loves you very very much.
Xxxxxxxxxxxxxxxxxxxxxxxxxxx

♡ ♡ ♡ ♡ ♡ ♡ ♡ ♡ ♡ ♡ ♡ ♡ ♡ ♡

It was much better than what Mr. Prickles had written, Jack had to admit. Perhaps it would work. Perhaps it wouldn't matter if she didn't believe Mr. Prickles had written it. Maybe she would just be so curious, she'd come to the county show anyway. Then, when he'd won the sprout competition, she'd be sure to make friends with him again.

They agreed that Jack would take the card home with him because he knew where his mum kept her stamps, and he had a post box right outside his house.

He managed to slip out of the house when his mum was making tea. He stood in front of the post box for ages, too scared to post it, in case it made everything worse. But then a little voice in his head told him to go for it. He waited for another voice to tell him not to, but it didn't so he pushed it in and ran back inside the house.

That night he told his mum he was tired and went up to bed early. He drew a picture of himself rubbing his tummy and saying 'yum' in a speech bubble, looking at a plate of steaming sprouts. He stroked Max between his ears and whispered, "What if we could make the sprouts *extra* tasty to make *extra* sure that Mr. Prickles wins?"

It took him ages to fall asleep because he was too excited, but just before he did, a zizz of light flashed across the duvet.

 draw here

Chapter 28

Jack wasn't surprised to find himself back underground in the sprout nursery. He was surprised to see worms in white coats, mixing things in test-tubes. Rodney was tasting the liquids in the test-tubes.

He shuffled over to them, holding out a test-tube. "Try this and guess what it is!"

Jack sniffed it. It smelled like rotten leaves. He took a tiny sip: it tasted like it too. He'd had it once before at a worm feast.

"Um, rotten leaves?"

"Perfect! Yes, it is. Well, it isn't really, it just tastes like rotten leaves. We're injecting the taste into his sprouts so that his are the tastiest ever!"

Jack groaned. Mr. Prickles would never win the Tastiest Vegetable competition with that disgusting flavour. If Mrs. Prickles did come, it was going to be a disaster.

"Can I try?" asked Sally.

Jack passed the test-tube to Sally and she took a small sip, spat it out and wrinkled her nose.

"Yuck!"

Rodney looked concerned. "Don't you like it?"

"Not really, Rodney," said Jack.

"Oh. Oh dear." Rodney's head drooped in disappointment. "We thought you'd be so impressed."

"Well, it's a great idea," added Jack hastily, "it's just, well, humans don't like rotten leaves."

"They don't?" Rodney looked surprised.

"No, silly! They'd rather eat normal sprouts than ones that taste of rotten leaves," said Sally.

"Oh," said Rodney again.

"I know!" Jack was bouncing up and down. "You need to make them taste of chocolate or toffee or mint choc ice-cream! That would be awesome! I'd eat tonnes of sprouts if they tasted of chocolate!"

"Can you do that?" asked Sally, her eyes glowing in the dark with excitement.

"Yes, no problem. You should have said before."

"Really?" asked Jack and Sally together, in amazement.

"Yes," said Rodney. He went back to the other worms in white coats, brought them into a huddle, gave them some instructions and soon they were all mixing, shaking and testing new ingredients in the test-tubes.

Jack and Sally waited. After a few minutes, Rodney shuffled over to them, carrying three test-tubes on a tray. He bowed carefully to Jack, still managing to hold the tray straight so nothing spilled, "Your Majesty, please try these."

Jack took the first test-tube and sipped from it. His eyes lit up. "Yum! Chocolate!" He took the next one, and had a bigger sip, "Even better! Mint choc-chip!" He was about to take the third test-tube, when Rodney stopped him.

"This is our extra special one. We call it 'Turbo Trump'."

"Can I try? Can I, please?" Sally was bobbing up and down. She'd already tried the others, after Jack, and she was licking her lips in anticipation.

Rodney shook his head. "No, sorry, this one is just for King Worm Jack to try. We don't have many supplies of this one."

Jack felt important again, and stood straighter, adjusted his crown and then took a tiny sip.

"Wow!" Jack felt the liquid tingle on his tongue. He felt the tiny drop of liquid fizz all the way down to his tummy, but then it kept on going, down to his toes (if worms had toes). A small but powerful fart escaped from Jack's bottom. He blushed and then he started to bounce, softly at first, then he couldn't resist doing a double backwards somersault. "Yay!" he cried. He did another somersault, then another, then...he stopped and flopped onto the ground.

"Amazing!"

"What's in that stuff?" asked Sally.

Rodney smiled, "It's a secret recipe, and supplies are so scarce, there will only be one sprout in every bunch that will taste like this."

Jack was standing up again, "I don't care about the taste! It's the feeling: it's amazing. It's like I can do anything — and I really wanted to do some somersaults."

"Can I try some? Please?" Sally was desperate to have a go.

"No, sorry," Rodney shook his head firmly.

 *draw here*

Jack winked at Sally, then whispered something to Rodney. Rodney frowned, but then he passed Jack a small pot and went back over to the other worms, and started to fill some syringes.

Jack held out the pot to Sally who stuck her finger in it and then licked it. Sally stood for a moment, let out a small but pungent fart, and then started doing somersaults down the tunnel. Jack tucked the pot inside his wormsie and followed, grinning.

Chapter 29

It was Friday, the day before the county show and Jack bounced into the classroom, impatient to get through the day. Hopefully, Mr. Prickles would do something fun outside again. He was sure that he'd also be excited about tomorrow. There was no way he'd set them boring worksheets to do. If he was anything like Jack when he was excited, he'd have too much jumpy energy to sit at his desk watching them work.

As soon as Mr. Prickles came into the classroom, Jack knew something terrible had happened. His stomach did somersaults. Not the happy kind. The shaky, sicky, anxious kind.

"Sit down and be quiet. NOW."

Jack and Sally shared a nervous glance and sat down with everyone else. The classroom was silent. Mr. Prickles stayed standing, he stared at them, his nostrils flared, he moved round in front of his desk, and he cracked his knuckles.

"Someone has been in my desk and stolen my private property."

Jack thought he might faint. He heard Sally gasp. He dropped his head and stared at the floor.

"That someone is sitting in my classroom. We are all going to wait here until that person or persons owns up."

Jack felt his cheeks flush. He risked a glance upwards and saw that Mr. Prickles was leaning against the front of his desk, facing them with his arms crossed, and his eyes narrowed. Jack sank lower into his chair.

"We have all day. For every minute that we wait, your lunchtime will reduce by the same number of minutes. For all of you."

His classmates started to mutter. If he sank much lower in his chair, he'd fall off it. He started to tremble.

Sally prodded him. He shook her off. She prodded him again and then whispered, "we have to own up."

He shook his head. They'd be in such big trouble.

He heard Sally clear her throat. He looked up straight into the glare of Mr. Prickles' narrowed eyes. An eyebrow twitched. Jack looked at Sally. She nodded.

In a tiny voice, Sally said, "It was us, Mr. Prickles."

Jack shut his eyes.

"US?" thundered Mr. Prickles.

Jack opened his eyes as he felt a heavy, threatening presence next to him. Mr. Prickles was standing by his chair. Time to own up.

"Y...yes, us, Mr. Prickles." he stuttered, "me and Sally."

The classroom was deathly silent.

"I see. You and Sally." His voice was so quiet, Jack flinched, waiting for the shouting that would follow. Instead, Mr. Prickles carried on in the same calm, quiet voice. "Up. Both of you. Up now. We're going to see the head." He raised his voice. "And the rest of you, I want absolute silence while I deal with these two."

Jack's knees were trembling as he followed Sally out of the classroom, with Mr. Prickles right behind him.

Chapter 30

It was the day of the county show. Jack was grounded. His mum had been furious. Neither his headteacher, Mrs. Root, nor his mum had understood that he and Sally were just trying to help.

Jack's whole family was going to the gala, because Seb was entering Scarlet into the Best Pet Trick competition. Even when Jack told his mum and dad that his cartoon strip had been entered into the show's creative writing competition, they wouldn't let him go. He hadn't told them he'd also entered Max into the Best Pet Trick competition. He was sure Max would win with his secret ingredient. Scarlet would look so rubbish next to Max and then Seb could never laugh at him again.

He had to go to the show, not just for the competitions, but to explain himself to Mr. Prickles. It wasn't fair that he was cross with him. He'd been trying to do a good thing. And he wanted to see how tasty the sprouts were. He was going, and no one was going to stop him.

The show was busy. Most of Jack's school seemed to be there. Jack slipped inside the vegetable tent and looked for the sprout section. He spotted Mr. Prickles, decided that he looked in a good mood and wandered over, casually, his hands in his pockets.

"Hello, Mr. Prickles."

"Jack."

They looked at each other. Jack scuffed his toe in the dirt. "I'm sorry. I was only trying to help."

"I know you were, Jack."

Jack looked at him in surprise. Mr. Prickles was smiling at him.

"It's just that, well, you seemed really sad, and we just...just wanted to help, and we knew if we could get your wife to come today, it would all be okay." He waited.

"Next time you want to do a good deed, just think about it a little more carefully. You shouldn't have been in my desk, and you shouldn't have read something that didn't belong to you."

Jack was confused. He couldn't work out if he was forgiven or not.

"Anyway, no harm done after all. Mrs. Prickles appears to think that the added comments were very well put. I am expecting her to make an appearance today."

Jack watched in amazement as Mr. Prickles blushed as red as strawberry jam.

"What do you think of these beauties?" Mr. Prickles turned to admire his sprouts.

If Mr. Prickles wasn't going to say any more about it, then neither would he. Jack looked at the sprouts, still on their stalk. They did look good — if you liked sprouts. They were big and glossy.

"They look great, Mr. Prickles."

Mr. Prickles rubbed his hands together. "I've never grown any that look like this before. I'm sure I'm going to win it this year."

His sprouts did look better than everyone else's, Jack thought. But the taste was more important than the look.

"Have you tasted them yet?"

"No, Jack. They looked so wonderful, I couldn't bring myself to pick any off the stalk. I can't wait to try them, though."

Each vegetable owner had a little camping stove, so that after the judges had scored the look of them, the owners could cook them up and then offer them to the judges for tasting.

"If I come back later, could I try one, when you've cooked them?"

Mr. Prickles beamed at Jack. "Of course you can, Jack."

"You see, I've got to go now because it's the Best Pet Trick competition in a minute, and I've entered my cat, Max."

Mr. Prickles looked surprised, "Oh, really?"

Jack carefully slipped his rucksack off his back, laid it on the ground and then unzipped it.

"Meow!" said Max as he stuck his head out and stretched, putting first one paw and then the other carefully on the grass. He stretched again, arching his back, and then stepped fully out of the rucksack.

 draw here

Mr. Prickles laughed. "I'll be crossing my fingers for you, Jack. What trick will he do?"

"Somersaults," announced Jack. "And if you see my parents, please could you tell them that you're not mad at me anymore and that I'm not in trouble?"

"I will. So long as you promise never to go rummaging in my desk again."

"I promise."

"Good luck then, Jack."

"Good luck to you, too, Mr. Prickles."

Jack scooped Max up and left the tent before Mr. Prickles could change his mind and decide to be mad at him again.

Chapter 31

They had to wait out of sight until it was time to check in for their slot. He really hoped his parents weren't going to be furious when they saw him here. He was hoping that they would be so amazed by Max, they'd forget that they'd grounded him.

The small pet category was just finishing when Jack walked over, with Max at his heels. There were mice, rats, hamsters and rabbits, all running round things, or through things. Jack yawned. Max stopped to wash his face. The small pets weren't very interesting.

Jack stood at the side, where he could see his mum and dad watching Seb. Seb and Scarlet were ready to kick off the medium pet category. Then they were off. Seb was attempting ten skips with Scarlet skipping with him. He managed fifteen and the crowd cheered. Even Jack clapped, because it was impressive. He could see his mum and dad were very impressed.

Then Jack's name was called. He glanced over to his mum and dad, noting their surprised expressions. They were going to be even more surprised in a minute. He and Max walked into the roped off area, where the tricks took place. Jack ignored the laughter that he could hear. He would show them how amazing Max was.

Jack crouched down next to Max. He felt in his pocket for the tiny pot of Turbo Trump and unscrewed the lid with one hand, leaving both pot and lid in his pocket, so no one could see. He took out some ham from his backpack and gave Max a piece, which he gobbled up. There were some jeers from the crowd.

"Come on, eating ham isn't a trick!"

"Get a proper pet on, to show us a trick!"

Jack ignored them. He took another piece of ham and pretended he was hiding it from Max in his pocket. Max jumped up onto his hind legs and tried to reach for Jack's pocket with his front paws.

Jack heard his brother yell from the side, "Come on, Jack. You can stop now. You don't have to do a trick, just because I dared you. Come on, get off!"

Jack smiled to himself as he dipped the corner of the piece of ham into the tiny pot, and then held it high for Max to jump up and snatch it out of his hand. There were a few cheers, but mostly laughter.

Then Jack smelt the unmistakeable stench of Max farting. It smelt like a rotting compost heap. Jack stood up, checked his parents were watching (they looked embarrassed, he thought) and then he clicked his fingers and shouted, "Go Max, go!"

Max meowed loudly, and Jack was sure he winked at him. Max leapt up from the ground straight above him into the air, did four forwards somersaults and landed. There was stunned silence and then the crowd erupted into cheers. Next, Max did three cartwheels in a row. Not just any old cartwheels, these were two-paw cartwheels, only his back paws touching the ground. Finally, to finish off his routine, Max ran, took off, did a pirouette in the air and landed in Jack's arms.

The crowd went wild. Jack's parents rushed into the roped-off area and flung their arms round Jack. Seb looked shocked. Scarlet had flopped onto the ground, with her head between her paws. Max rubbed his nose affectionately into Jack's chest. He was the best cat ever.

Chapter 32

As Jack and Max were being awarded their winner's rosette, Sally came running over.

"Jack! Jack!" You have to come to the creative writing tent! Come on!"

"Why?"

"It's your cartoon! You've got a certificate!"

As soon as Jack had the rosette, he snatched up his rucksack, grabbed Max and ran. Seb and Scarlet stayed where they were, sulking. Jack pushed through the crowd of children and parents and there was his cartoon strip, with a 'Highly Commended' certificate next to it. Sally's had won first prize.

Just for a moment he felt a pang of jealousy, but then his mum arrived and squeezed all the air out of him with a huge bear hug.

"Jack, you really are a wonder! First Max, then this. That's brilliant!" His mum beamed at him.

Jack squinted up at her. "So, you're not mad at me then?"

"No, we're not mad at you. Slightly cross still perhaps, but not mad."

His dad appeared at her side and ruffled his hair, smiling at him. "Mr. Prickles has just been over to explain. You're daft, but we're proud of you for trying to help Mr. Prickles. Your intention was good, even if what you did was wrong."

Max, who was still in Jack's arms, meowed loudly and tried to headbutt his dad. They all laughed.

"And I'm not sure how you managed to get Max to do those amazing somersaults, and as for your cartoon here...well, that's just brilliant, Jack." His dad looked really genuinely happy for him. With any luck neither parent was going to mention that he was supposed to be grounded.

"Yeah, Jack, that's epic!" Sally was jigging up and down next to him.

Jack nodded at Sally, "Thanks. Well done, too. First prize is amazing."

She grinned from ear to ear, with her parents standing proudly behind her. He was pleased for Sally, but he couldn't help feeling sad that it wasn't *his* parents being proud of a first prize.

He whispered to his mum, "Are you proud of me, Mum?"

His mum squeezed him tight again and whispered back, "Yes, of course I am, Jack, very proud. You don't need to win prizes to make me proud. You're perfect just the way you are. Well, I mean when you're not sneaking around the classroom stealing your teacher's cards." She grinned at him, so he knew she wasn't really cross.

It was all Jack had ever wanted to hear. He wondered if Mrs. Prickles had arrived yet and was proud of Mr. Prickles, too. "Come on," he shouted to everyone, "we have to go to the vegetable tent now."

There was quite a commotion in the tent when they got there. Jack pushed his way to the front of the crowd and emerged to see Mr. Prickles looking confused but proud. He'd just won first prize. The judges were still gobbling down his sprouts.

"Amazing!"

"Delicious!"

"Hints of velvety chocolate. Fantastic!"

"Mint, no — chocolate — no, it's both. Mint choc chip!"

"How does he do it?"

"Incredible!"

The local news reporter had thrust a microphone in front of Mr. Prickles, "Tell us, how did you achieve these magnificent flavours?"

"Um, I don't know, really," said Mr. Prickles, which was very truthful, thought Jack. "I suppose I just nurtured them, took good care of them. They seemed to blossom in the last week."

"Have you eaten one yet, Mr. Prickles?"

"Well, actually, no. They seemed to go very quickly once the judging started." A couple of the judges tried to blend into the crowd behind them.

"I've saved two though, one for a certain young man who I'm sure will now love sprouts for life," and he winked at Jack and passed one to him, "and one for me, which I shall try now."

Jack had already eaten his and the chocolate flavour was lingering deliciously on his tongue. Mr. Prickles popped his into his mouth and chewed. He shut his eyes, appearing to savour the moment and then his eyes snapped open and there was just the tiniest explosive fart.

His eyes shone. He grinned from ear to ear, and then he did three back flips as the crowd quickly moved, to give him space. He stood up tall and raised his hands into the air as the crowd cheered.

Then a short woman with long, wavy, chestnut-coloured hair stepped forward and Jack heard a sharp intake of breath next to him.

"It's her! I bet that's his wife!"

Sally was standing next to Jack. Max meowed and rubbed himself against her legs.

Mr. Prickles took a step towards Mrs. Prickles and then she grabbed him and planted a huge kiss on his lips. Jack and Sally looked away quickly.

"Yuck!" said Jack.

"Eugh!" said Sally.

Mr. Prickles looked up and saw them. Then, holding his wife's hand, with a huge smile on his face, he walked over to them.

"Ah, Jack, Sally and Mr. and Mrs. Wrigglesworth. May I present my wife, Judy Prickles?"

They all shook hands.

"I saw your amazing cat show, Jack. Incredible!"

Jack blushed, "Thanks, Mrs. Prickles."

"Mr. Prickles' sprouts were amazing too!" blurted Sally.

"So I hear," said Mrs. Prickles, gazing up at Mr. Prickles.

Jack hoped they weren't going to start kissing again.

"It's almost as if your cartoon strip came true, Jack," said Mr. Prickles, staring closely at Jack, with a quizzical look on his face.

"He got a Highly Commended, Mr. Prickles! And I won first prize!"

"I know, Sally. In fact, my lovely wife remarked on what wonderful creative writing skills my pupils have."

Mrs. Prickles winked at them, "Yes, some very persuasive writing skills."

Jack and Sally looked at each other and grinned.

Without taking his eyes off his wife, Mr. Prickles smiled and said, "Well, if you'll excuse us, Mrs. Prickles and I have a lot of catching up to do."

Chapter 33

Jack was exhausted that night. It had been an amazing day. Mr. Prickles was very happy. He was back with his wife *and* he'd won the Tastiest Vegetable competition. And Max had won the Best Pet Trick competition. And he, Jack, had won a certificate for his cartoon strip. Who'd have thought it? Mrs. Prickles was proud of Mr. Prickles. And Jack's mum had said how proud she was of him. It was all perfect. And he wasn't in trouble anymore. The perfect plan, like Sally had said.

The only person who was grumpy now was Seb. He'd have to think of a way to cheer him up. Later, though. He wanted to enjoy this moment.

Jack stroked Max. "I'd better let Rodney know all the good news. We should celebrate with a worm feast!"

Max winked, and a flash of light zizzed across the duvet.

Acknowledgements

The biggest thank you goes to Adrian, Millie and Isla for their contributions, support and encouragement along the way. Thanks also to the Lancaster Creative Writing MA group for their feedback at an early stage. Special thanks to Janet Lees, the best writing buddy I could wish for. To Evan Clement for asking to illustrate an earlier version, and giving me the idea for do-it-yourself illustrations. To Lucy Frontani and team at Scotforth Books for the care they've taken to bring King Worm Jack to you, the reader. And, finally, to Ivan Frontani for somehow translating the images inside my head into brilliant illustrations!